Ann Schweninger

Off to School!

Viking Kestrel

For Marilee Robin Burton

Grateful acknowledgment is made to Frederick Warne & Co.
for permission to reprint an excerpt from *The Tale of Peter Rabbit*,
by Beatrix Potter.

The artwork was rendered on Arches watercolor paper with watercolor washes,
ink, carbon pencil, and colored pencil. The artist used a size 00 paintbrush
and a Hunt 104 crow-quill pen point.

VIKING KESTREL
Viking Penguin Inc., 40 West 23rd Street, New York, New York 10010, U.S.A.
Penguin Books Ltd, Harmondsworth, Middlesex, England
Penguin Books Australia Ltd, Ringwood, Victoria, Australia
Penguin Books Canada Limited, 2801 John Street, Markham, Ontario, Canada L3R 1B4
Penguin Books (N.Z.) Ltd, 182–190 Wairau Road, Auckland 10, New Zealand

Copyright © Ann Schweninger, 1987
All rights reserved
First published in 1987 by Viking Penguin Inc.
Published simultaneously in Canada
Printed in Japan by Dai Nippon Printing Co. Ltd.
Set in Windsor Light.
1 2 3 4 5 91 90 89 88 87

Library of Congress Cataloging in Publication Data
Schweninger, Ann.   Off to school!
Summary: Button Brown has an exciting first day at
school as he and his classmates play games, draw
pictures, have a snack, and hear a story.
[1. Schools—Fiction] I. Title.
PZ7.S412630f 1987   [E]   86-26736   ISBN 0-670-81447-4

Getting Ready

Going to School

Names, Names

Playground

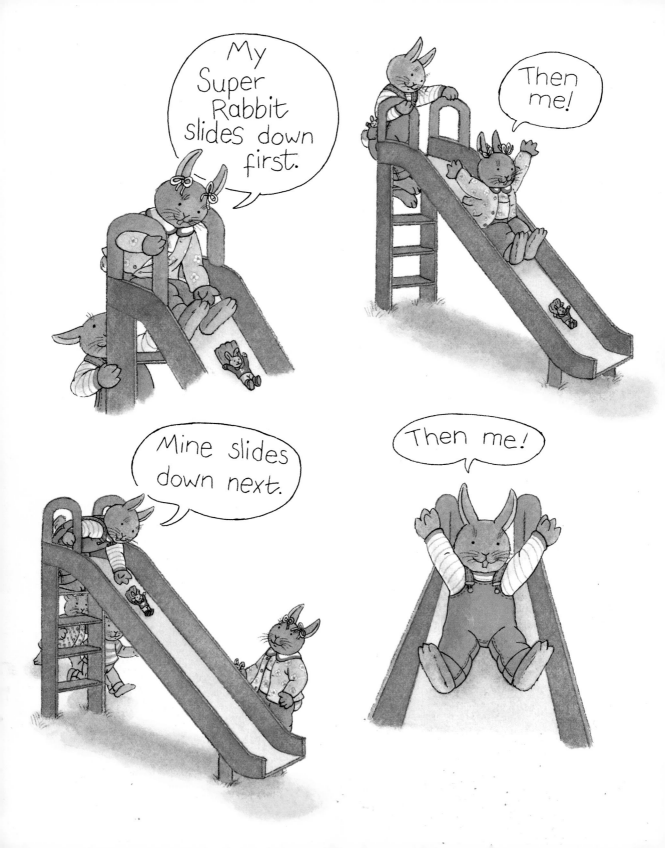

Ring around the Rosie,
A pocket full of posies,
Ashes, ashes!

We all fall down!

Alphabet and Storytime

After School